CW00857285

Golden Crystal
Palace

Amy Louise Rickard

Copyright © 2019 by Amy Louise Rickard. 784572

All rights reserved. No part of this book may
be reproduced or transmitted in any form or by
any means, electronic or mechanical, including
photocopying, recording, or by any information
storage and retrieval system, without permission
in writing from the copyright owner.

This is a work of fiction. Names, characters,
places and incidents either are the product of the
author's imagination or are used fictitiously, and
any resemblance to any actual persons, living or
dead, events, or locales is entirely coincidental.

To order additional copies of this book, contact:
Xlibris
1-800-455-039
www.xlibris.com.au
Orders@Xlibris.com.au

ISBN: Softcover   978-1-7960-0828-9
         EBook   978-1-7960-0827-2

Print information available on the last page

Rev. date: 11/21/2019

Maykalia, Blair and the Golden Crystal Palace

Amy Louise Rickard

I would like to thank everyone who has helped me along the way.

I dedicate this book to my best friend, Michael James Skipworth.
I love you for your bravery and your courage in the life you lived.

I also dedicate it to my Dad, Norman Heath Rickard. Thanks for all you are, Dad and everything you have done for me over the years.

Finally, I would like to dedicate this book to my children, Adam, Jake, Max and Chloe. My world wouldn't be the same without you guys. I love my children; no one can take a love between a child and a Mum. It is pure.

Once upon a time in the kingdom of Adrella lived a King and Queen, Blair and Maykalia.

Raging unicorns in frosent light, comes a Golden
Crystal Palace with delight.

Inside the Golden Crystal Palace, the Ballroom had golden crystals in the lights.

Blair and Maykalia used to dance away the night.

Outside the ocean spray came floating up. Seahorses and starfish played in rock pools. A Lighthouse sat high up on a hill, overlooking the waves that crashed down onto the golden sand, with lights that lit up the whole town late at night…

And guided the Fishermen in their tracks.

Back at the Golden Crystal Palace, Blair and Maykalia are in the horses stables. Jenna is having her foals, Star and Blaze. They lie quietly by her side in the sunset sky.

When Blair and Maykalia arrived back to the Golden Crystal Palace, there was another princess in the castle. Maykalia flew off into a jealous rage.

She ran into the Forest. Night was about to fall and as she leaned down she could see white rabbits and a creek amongst the trees. She curled up and fell asleep.

The king, Blair, tried to find her. He called out for Maykalia in the darkness of the Forest.

He even took his horse but there was no luck. So he went back to the Golden Crystal Palace.

He said, "Forever your dreams; let them soar away into the night."

As he said these words, red dragons flew over the Queen of Adrella and released red and black fireballs into the darkness of the night.

Back at the Golden Crystal Palace, the golden ducks and the swans floated around, comfort in the darkness of the night.

Maykalia awoke up from her sleep. There was a huge rainbow in the sky. She turned around and saw Blair. He was standing just behind her, under the rainbow-filled sky.

"What happened to the other princess?" Maykalia asked.

"She was only here to help with Star and Blaze. She is a Horse Trainer. You're the girl of my dreams and no one will ever come close," Blair said to Maykalia. "I would love you to return to the Golden Crystal Palace with me."

When they got back, there were golden and black balloons and hundreds of roses filling the room. The lights were dimmed.

Blair turned to Maykalia. "We are celebrating your return tonight with a party in our Crystal Ballroom," he said.

About the Author

I, Amy Louise Rickard, was born and grew up in Balwyn in Melbourne, Australia.

From a young girl I always liked telling stories to my sister.

When I was in year 10 at Methodist Ladies' College in Perth, my English teacher said she enjoyed my stories that I had written and one day I should write stories.

In 2018 I studied an evening course in creative writing at Sydney University's Centre for Continuing Education. Through this course I wrote my own book.

I hope you all enjoy reading my story, *Maykalia, Blair and the Golden Crystal Palace*.

In summertime I enjoy family time with my four children: Adam, twins Jake and Max and Chloe. We like to swim at the beach in the waves.

CPSIA information can be obtained at www.ICGtesting.com
Printed in the USA
BVIW120450291119
565083BV00003B/17

WITHIN THESE WALLS

BY

NARI

Illustrations By: Orlando Walker

Copyright © 2019 by Nari. 793037

All rights reserved. No part of this book may
be reproduced or transmitted in any form or by
any means, electronic or mechanical, including
photocopying, recording, or by any information storage
and retrieval system, without permission in writing from
the copyright owner.

To order additional copies of this book, contact:
Xlibris
1-888-795-4274
www.Xlibris.com
Orders@Xlibris.com

ISBN: 978-1-7960-6292-2 (sc)
ISBN: 978-1-7960-6291-5 (e)

Print information available on the last page

Rev. date: 09/30/2019

Within These Walls

by

Nari

illustrations by

Orlando Walker

DEDICATION PAGE

For women that have been sexually silenced and suppressed. We have been made to feel ashamed for something that is supposed to be natural and dominated by societal norms for too long! I speak on your behalf. We are sexual creatures with thoughts and desires parallel to those of men. Today, I break the shackles of stigmas and release the power within our walls! To my circle of supportive friends and family, I want to personally thank you for cheering and encouraging me to bravely speak the truth.

Special Thanks to Orlando Walker for taking on a project that was Unapologetic & Raw and capturing the very element of my thoughts. I am eternally grateful for you bringing life to my words. Special Thanks to Billz Productions for capturing me in a space that reveals my inner sexual goddess. Last but certainly not least; R.P. – The inspiration I draw from you is beyond priceless!

TABLE OF CONTENTS

Chapter 1 1

    Within these Walls 2

    Within These Walls Part II 4

    Infatuated 6

    Naughty Morning Thoughts of You.. 8

    Clarification 9

    She knows... 10

    She is... 12

    My Lips 13

    Caramel Dream 15

    House Calls 17

    When??? 19

    My little Secret 20

Chapter 2 21

    With Just One Look... 22

    Surrendering Came Easy 24

    Love It When You... 25

    13 Minutes (Part 1) 27

    Something About The Way You.. 29

    Caramel Love 31

    13 Minutes Part II 32

    Morning Talk With My Pussy.. 33

    Designed by Desire 34

    Anticipation 35

    Wet 36

    Take me back 37

    Drip 38

    April Mornings 39

    Slurping On It... 40

    Big. Beautiful. Woman 41

    Pussy on Toast 43

    When You Get Here.. 44

CHAPTER 1

"The Journey To Rediscovery"
(CREAM IN MY COFFEE)

After years of holding back; Nari embarks on a new journey as she examines her past sexual endeavors. She reflects on her most memorable experiences and draws from them. Nari partakes in the exploration of her body and rediscovers her most intimate pleasures.

Within these Walls

Within these Walls
Is warmth
Wetness
And unlimited pleasure

Within these walls
Your girth increases
Heart races
And you're covered in lust

Within these walls
Are Sinful thoughts
Passionate Desires
Pleasurable Actions

Within these walls
You are Swaddled
In Gushy Greatness
Until you release …

Within these walls
I hold you close
Create a rhythm
And ride until neither of us can speak

Within these walls
You grew
Until you couldn't rise anymore
You were taken to your peak

Within these walls
Is a place
Where we communicate -
Telepathically

Within these walls
Our minds and bodies behold our words
Our Silence Speaks Volumes -
That is never heard

Within these walls
Our language is understood
Nobody else can get under my hood
Or paint these walls the way you can

Within these walls
You are - more than a man!
You're the satisfaction
To my every desire

Within these walls - You're the human form
Of actual pleasure
My "Magic Stick"
My Ultimate Sexual Endeavor

Within these walls
I yearn for you to be
Devouring every inch
Of this Warm, Moist Luxury!

Within These Walls Part II

Within these walls
I want to wine on you
Wrap my legs around your waist
And slow grind on you

Make your body do things
You never knew it could do
Slide inside of me
Let me show you

Within these walls
Goodness flows like a waterfall
In this Beautiful Wetness
You stand firm and tall

Within these walls
I want you to
Feel, touch
And See

Within these walls
You'll reach a destination
Where you'll truly meet me
As I will meet you

Within these walls
We will blend together as one
Our waters will intertwine
And now we are done

Within these walls
I have pleased you
You have pleased me
Within these walls we've reached Ecstasy!

Infatuated

Got me lying awake in the midst of the night
Thinking bout the way you lick
Mmm....Your lips
My lips

The way we kiss (la forma en que nos besamos)
And how you glance up at me
With that sparkle of sexy in your eyes
Damn!!!

Juices is dripping down my thighs
I'm wrapped up
In pleasure - as I
Caress on your ears

You make me tingle all over and I forget all of my fears
All I can feel in this moment is you
Thrusting inside of me
Me bouncing all over that dick

Periodic flashbacks got me randomly smiling
In the middle of the day,
Night
Even in my sleep

Thinking about you makes me tingle - Real Deep
In places I didn't know could be reached
You've turned me on and ignited a fire
Until we meet again, I'll be filled with desire! (hasta que nos
encontremos de Nuevo, estare llena de deseo!!)

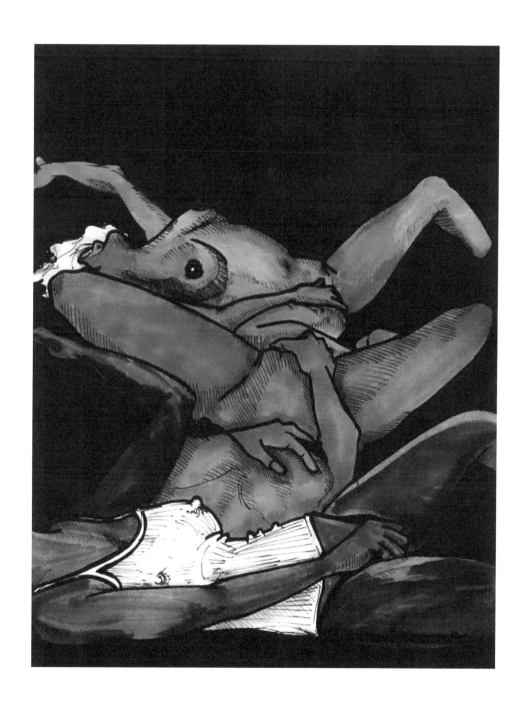

Naughty Morning Thoughts of You...

As the head of your dick enters my pussy
She welcomes him with a hug
Snug, warm and gushy
He backs up and re - enters
And is embraced repeatedly by her overflowing of joy, desire and pleasure

I can feel heat gently caressing my spine
As our bodies intertwine
And we thrust, wine, moan and grind
All over one another

Wrapped up in ecstasy
I'm biting my lip,
You're touching my clit
In multiple ways and I'm ready to explode but I don't want this to end

So we change positions
Let's do this again
On my neck from behind, you softly kiss
Making me sooooo wet
That my juices are running down my thighs

You begin to grab and slap my ass
Oh My! Now I'm really turned on
I mean ready to blow
At this point,
However you want it - is where we'll go
I've lost all control
you've taken over me
Feels so damn good
I can't even see

We've both reached our climax
As we lye in awe
All I can think about is
When? When do I get more?

Clarification

Trying to wrap my mind around your confusion
Wondering how you came up with such a deep illusion
But I get it - You've been dealing with them unfamiliar, uncertain girls

Here's where I want your mind to whirl
Around the fact that "I am not them"
And they are "not me"
The woman I am is rarely seen

See I'm familiar with myself
In many different ways
I can do it alone
But I prefer when you - play

With my body
And make me fluster with joy
And I'm absolutely, positively Certain
That you - I enjoy!

My mind is not weak
Or easily swayed
Two worlds I separate
No time for dismay

This thing we got
It's strictly for pleasure
The orgasms you give me
Are beyond measure

Let me keep riding, sliding, sucking, grinding - on that dick
While you Keep kissing all over me and licking my clit
No complications, we're both here for the same shit! (Pleasure)

She knows...

Exactly what she wants
when she walks into a room
Yeah that's sex in her eyes
And they're looking at - you

Thinking about how
She's gonna- Take You Down
Climb up on top of you
And move her hips all around

She knows just how good it tastes
All she can think of is seeing it in her face
Thickening and Rising with every lick
Imagining the ERUPTION of that Dick!

Naughtily -
She smiles at you
From across the room
Knowing that you want to please her too

As she walks, her hips sway
To the rhythm of your bodies intertwined
Taken over by thoughts of you
She knows that her mind

Is completely captivated by the things you do
She knows just how to get to you
So you can do the things she likes
So play along and make this - An Amazing Night!

She is...

More than a woman
She's a Sexual Being
A Caramel Goddess
Seductive Queen

Pride she takes in every performance
Leaving it all on the stage
A naughty prowess
All she needs is a cage

Under the spotlight,
She'll dominate
But she won't be confined
From the bars she'll break free

Leaving a trail
Of Caramel kisses behind
More than beautiful
She's "Summertime Fine"

Taking the world by storm
Letting her Sexy run free
She is I
And I am - She!

My Lips

My lips
Crave the touch of yours
Gently sucking on them
As you sensually

Tease me
With your tongue,
Caress me
With your hands

My Lips
Enthusiastically prepare
To press
Against the soft, juicy-ness of yours

Barely containing their excitement
To encounter your skin
And travel
Along the journey that is your body

My Lips
Ache to feel the piercing
Of your tip
Longggg - to feel you Penetrate

The entrance
Of my secret tunnel
Desire to open up
To embrace your arrival

My Lips
Have never had A pleasure such as you
They are delighted to take part
In all - that you will do

To ignite
My inner flame
Tame
My wild desires

These Lips - My Lips
Are sensual,
Sexual
Enticing and True

These Lips - My Lips
Were made to Devour You!

Caramel Dream

I love when I step into a room and you
Are taken a back
Flustered by the way I lack-
Bashfulness

Confidently gliding across the floor
You glance me over from head to toe
Mentally Devouring Me
And already wanting more

Even though we have yet to begin
Got you blushing
Thinking about it
On your face there's a grin

The look of desire,
Look of fantasy
I came prepared
To make you -Cum for me

You seem to like this little thing I'm wearing
As it falls to the floor
Your clothes - I'm tearing

As we become one
In intimacy
And in nature
Our bodies create a mesmerizing flavor

My sugar & vanilla
Mixed with your butter & cream
Got us floating on clouds
In this Caramel Dream!

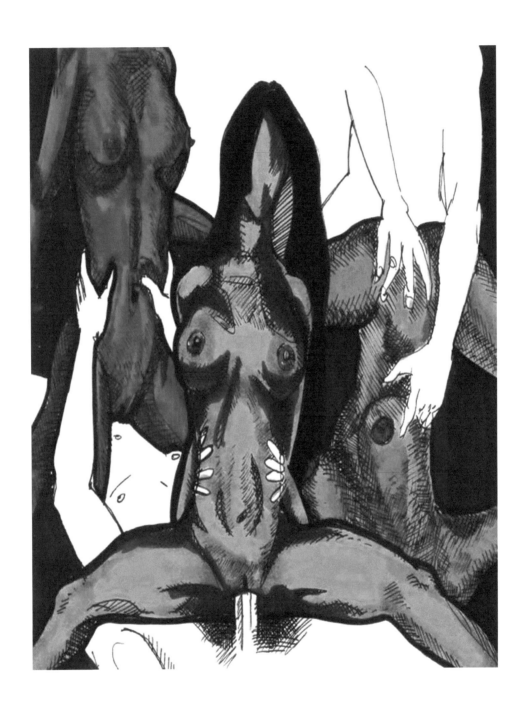

House Calls

Coconut oil, perfume & candles
Lingerie, pumps, & a pinch of Dominance
Go into my bag
As I prepare

To
Make this House Call
Step into your presence
Make your eyes fall

To the floor
As they watch me
Slowly they rise
And gently they stare

Knowing that I've come to
Take Care
Of you
And all of your minds desires

Came here to -
Deliver my A Game
Tame your inner beast
Put out your flaming fire

See my House Calls
Can change your life
I bring the liquids
That flow down your pipe

The care that I give
Will take your breath away
I'll resuscitate you
Then continue to play

Bring your body to places
You didn't know it could go
Kiss you passionately
At the exact moment you blow!

Stare deep in your eyes
While gently sucking on your balls
When I come to visit
I'm giving you my All!

Don't you want me to make a House Call?

When???

"When are you coming to get this bomb ass dick?" He said

Now I can't get these thoughts out of my head
I'm on my way
Get it ready for me
Wanna ride it so bad - I can barely see
Anything except flashing images of me straddling over you

Hoping you're thinking about me too
Yearning to devour all of it
Salivating as I think of it piercing my lips

Internally quivering with desire
I can hardly contain my thoughts
My Thighs are shaking
Mind is racing
I'm contemplating

Walking in, pinning you up against the wall
Never making it to the bed
Taking you in while you stand tall

Wrapping my legs around your waist
My ass cheeks resting in the palms of your hands
Put your back into it - Now I'm in a trance

Thinking about your thickness in the middle of the day
When?
Am I coming to get that Bomb Ass Dick you say
I'm Cumming Right Now!
I'm on my way...

My little Secret

That thing that has me smiling
From the inside out
I'm glowing

Thinking about you (pensando en ti)
All the little things you do
That I like
That turn me on

Forbidden things Nasty, Naughty things Guilty pleasures
Got me blushing & beaming beyond measure

Contemplating all
Of the things
I want to do
to you

My little secret
Where I go creeping
Seeking satisfaction
That surpasses my desires

The way I put it on you (La forma en que te penetro)
And you put it on me
There is nowhere else
I'd rather be

Than near you,
"On" you
And you
"In"me

Forever my
Sexy
Sinful
Secret- is what you'll be!

CHAPTER 2

"She's Backkk"
(The Cosmopolitan)

Right back like she never left; Nari has found herself. The sexual goddess within has shown up and is showing out. She refuses to be a version of societal sexual norms. Nari is taking charge and showing the world that being a "Lady" and a "Sexual Creature" are simultaneous acts. She's not holding back on her thoughts, needs or desires. She's speaking bold and freely about sex. Nari is commanding sexual empowerment for herself and all women.

With Just One Look

The grins
Giggles,
Butterflies
The weakness in my knees
It all came rushing back to me

The grins
Giggles,
Butterflies
The weakness in my knees

With just one look
You've got me mesmerized
Got me feeling hot
Between my thighs

With just one look
I'm excited
Turned on
Ready to obey your every command

With just one look
You're turned on
Fire ignited
Ready to "STAND"

With just one look
We find ourselves
Right back
Where we used to be

With just one look
It is clear to see
That I desire you
And you desire me!

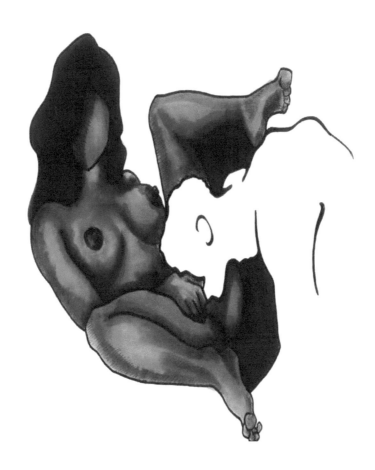

Surrendering Came Easy

Surrendering came easy simply because the door is locked and I'm alone

My day was tense and images of you flash in my mind

Simply because I have this silk dress on and it feels like you

-Smells like me

The two together is an overpowering seduction

Surrendering came easy simply because my thigh is smooth like your chest

I feel the warmth as my hand approaches the prize

Surrendering came easy simply because they are gone and I have to take this

Opportunity before they return

Before the bells rings
Before the door opens
Before I lose my mind, I'll surrender All

All I have is on the line, moving towards that peak

That greatness that you indulge me in

I thought I'd give myself a little piece of Heaven until I reach you again

So here I sit, alone - smiling, dripping wet and thinking of you!

In the event I'm caught - I'll simply say: Surrendering Came Easy!!!

Love It When You...

Love it when you decide to let your imagination take control

When you pull out the props and play games that childhood could've never created

When strawberries and peaches become the most delightful fruits ever

Love it when you make me forget that "spankings" were supposed to be a bad thing

Love it when your tongue hits the strangest places and make my body tremble

—Dance
-Squirt Out Lovely Juices

Love it even more when my pussy throbs
-Craves you

And you:
Grab my waist from behind
Bend me across the stove
And Fill me with your Thickness

Feels like Heaven in Every Thrust
And I Love it!

13 Minutes (Part 1)

In thirteen minutes I can:
Open the door,
Slowly extend my leg,

Then slightly bend at the knees
As I roll my hips toward the backside
Then I'll gracefully - sit on it

"It" being the seat because I have 12 minutes and 23 seconds left to:
-Shut the door
Press the lock
Push the seat back, lowering it until you are facing the sun - roof

With 11 minutes and 34 seconds on the clock
I will sensually fling my right leg over the arm rest
Planting my stiletto heel on the drivers window
Arch my back and aggressively enjoy the pleasures of you!

At 6 minutes and 13 seconds remaining:
You are mind boggled
- tongue tied
- Standing At Attention!

Five minutes is not a lot of time no room for:

-Four play
-Small talk
-Or Breast Licking

So I grab it:
-Take it
Sit on it
Get a Good Mount and - Ride It!

Like a sex crazed maniac
-Wining
-Rolling
-Pumping All Over It!

Back Arched
Ass Hiked in the air
Moving like an untamed beast!

At the end of 13 minutes,
Time Cum's Flowing Like A River!!!

Something About The Way You...

There is:
Something about the way you
Set your eyes upon my hips,
Sway them - without movement

Imagination displays in your eyes
Showing me - taking you - down
Looks of 2 minute undressing's
Forces me to shyly smile

From across the room
You call with your strength
- I answer

Silhouette on the wall displays
Your hands behind your head
As you lay; My legs straddled over you
1 Hand in the air

I ride til my legs are numb
Heart is beating at a rate
Equivalent to speed itself
And you - just smile!

There is something about the way
You say so much - without a word
Tell me that I'm your midnight's craving
Mornings nourishment
Last meal!

Chocolate skin whispers to me- I answer
Taste is not an option, I want to
No! I "Need" to devour you
Chocolate is delicious
Especially with nuts!

There is something about the way
-You caress my ass with your mind
Yet - I know
-Feel the soft touch of your hands
All the while wondering if you can read my thoughts???

There is something about the way you...
-Just know when my silence says: "Come to me"

The way you answer when my body says: "I want; No I Need" you to
-Grab me
-Fling me
-Slap my Ass
-Pull my hair and give me the reality of the images in my head

There is something about you- that turns me ON!!!

Caramel Love

When I put this lovin' on you
I want you to taste it
Feel it
Be wrapped up in it

When I put this lovin' on you
I want the cream & sugar I'm made of
To stick to your tongue
And pleasure your taste buds

When I put this caramel lovin' on you
I want you to feel it melt in your mouth
Feel its smoothness in your hands
I want you to feel my excitement and understand

That this sweetness
Is one of a kind
It will fulfill your every need
And blow your mind

This caramel lovin
Will form a curl in your toes
A roll in your eyes
Make you explode

This Caramel Lovin
Is patient too
Perfecting its sweetness
Preparing for you!

13 Minutes Part II

All I need is 13 minutes,
Make sure these car doors are locked
We're in - A dimly lit area,
So nobody can see this car rock!

When you recline my seat,
My heels thump upon the dashboard
Our bodies meet - intimately
And the windows begin to fog up from the heat!

Down to minute 11
You've gone down and I'm in Heaven
Moaning and Floating on a cloud
Holding back don't want to be too
Loud

Now we're down to minute 6
Time for me to get my fix
Sliding down your chest my tongue goes
As you brace yourself for my embrace

When I take you in
You can barely move
We can't stop now
don't mess up this groove

Now we've arrived at minute 4
I push you back and take in more
Just as you start to lose your shit
I sit on it and make you flip

You're banging on the seat and slapping my ass
Biting on your bottom lip
Giving me them bedroom eyes
Just as we embark upon the prize

We shake and quiver
No words to say
Smile and exhale
Our time is done for today!

Morning Talk With My Pussy

Good Morning Beautiful
All night long
I've been thinking of you

Overflowing with joy
From the pleasure you bring me
Rather playing alone or with a toy

With perfection you complete every task
But a favor of you
I must ask

When I arch my back
I need you to contract
Your walls - vigorously

I need you to squeeze
the life from his eyes
Make him Moan and Plead

For mercy because he can't bare anymore
Squirt your juices all over him
Reveal what you have in store

Show him who you are
What you're capable of
My Dear Sweet Pussy, with you-
Make him fall in love!

Designed by Desire

A Blueprint for a Seductive Goddess
Blessed with Class
Grace, Beauty
And an Intriguing Ass

Designed to captivate
Slay, Slaughter
To Motivate
Penetrate leaving her mark in your mind

Designed by Desire
For all the world to see
But created for only you
To put out the fire in me

Designed to clear the floor
Shake the crowd
Hypnotize the room
To say no words yet speak extremely loud

Built with pleasure
Molded with grace
Kissed with caramel
Sprinkled with just the right taste

Designed by Desire
Chiseled with thought
Filled with your wildest dreams
Yet- Easily taught

To please you
Adjust to the things you need me to be
Designed by Desire
Created just for you

To do all the things you desire me to do!

Anticipation

Anticipation is real
Got me blushing
Gushing
Over the way you make me feel

Mind wondering about
All the possibilities
The naughty & nasty
Things you'll do to me

My Body trembles
At the thought
Of all the new things
I'm going to learn

All the spankings
That I've rightfully earned
Butterflies take over
With every passing thought

Anticipation is real
As real as 6:54 am poetry
I'm up thinking about you
You're sleep; dreaming about me

This waiting game
Increases my desire
Intensifies my fantasies
Ignites my inner fire

When I finally reach you
And you touch me
What an explosive moment
It will be

Anticipation is real- You'll see!

Wet

R & B in the rain
Thunder roaring from the sky
That's how wet I get
When he walks by (cuando el pasa cerca de mi)

Faucet water running
Ocean waves flowing
That's how wet I get
When he starts blowing

On the nape of my neck
On the back of my thigh
Soaking wet is what I get
Whenever he's nearby

Rivers Cascading
Fountains Spraying
That's how wet I get
Whenever he's slaying

This pussy to death
Beating it up
Then putting it to rest
That's how -wet -I -get

Volcanoes erupting
Rainforests Pouring
That's how wet I get
When he's exploring

All of me
And I am learning all of him (yo estoy aprendiendo to do de el)
Desire, Passion, Pleasure- A triple threat
Guaranteed to make me Wet!

Take me back

To that moment
When you did that thing
That made me tingle
In my most intimate place

Take me back
To the point
Where you speechlessly spoke volumes
About all the things you wanted to do - Loud & Clear

Take me back
To the minute
When you undressed me
With your eyes
And my nakedness awaited

Take me back
To the second
My body anticipated
Your entrance
And you penetrated my soul

Take me back
To the very moment
When the strokes intensified
When my walls wrapped around you
And the juices erupted from our bodies !

Drip

Drip goes the pussy
On site of you
Drip goes the pussy
Thinking bout the things you do

Drip goes the pussy
At the touch of your hand
Drip goes the pussy
When that thick dick stands

Drip goes the pussy
When she's riding that dick
Drip goes the pussy
When you give her a lick

Drip goes the pussy
As you smack that ass
Drip goes the pussy
But she does it with class

Drip goes the pussy
As she massages away
Drip goes the pussy
For you anytime - Night or Day! (Para ti a cualquier hora dia o noche)

April Mornings

As the sun rises
Adrenaline rushes through my body
She tingles in unseen places
Pressure Rises
Heart races

Warm air brushes across my skin
Awakening the sensuality in me
As my Nipples stiffen
I visualize
Begin to feel things with my eyes

Envisioning you
That Long - Thick Blessing
And the way it stands
At Attention for me
And at my command

Suddenly my body feels flush
Thighs are turning red
As I think about your thrust
Kitty tickled Pink as can be
Thinking of the way you put it on me

Every time you touch my body
It takes me back in time
To a place where my body is longing
Feenin', Wanting, Craving -
Those April Mornings!

Slurping On It

Slurp!
Stroke, twist
Slide down, Suck up

Lick, lick, lick
Tease the tip
Then take - it –all- in

Mmmm…
Mmmm …hmmm…
Slurping,
Sucking
Simultaneous Moaning

I guess it feels as good to you
As it tastes to me
Juices dripping
Lips catching every drop

Hands Twisting and Stroking
Mouth damn near choking
But I keep going
Because the more intense I suck
Your eyes keep rolling

You're loudly moaning
Giving me incentive
To keep going
Until you can't take No- More

I- Keep going until
You're ready to give
It all to me
To penetrate my soul
To Please Me!

Big. Beautiful. Woman .

Let me sit back and unwind
Contemplate how much you can handle
While I sip on this wine

See, I'm not sure if you can take all of me
I'm a Big Beautiful Woman
With a Fat, Juicy Pussy!

Are you ready for what I have in store?
For all of this pussy
And a whole lot more!

See I come with hips
Dimples, Curves
And Lipsssss!

I'm not just speaking of those on my face
All 4 of em' are succulent, scrumptious
You'll see - when you taste!

Oh... and babyyyy - do I have thick thighs
Tender yet strong enough
To save lives!

I'm a Big Beautiful Woman, yeah that's me
When you open this wrapper
There's a lot to see!

I got Ass for days
Big squishy cheeks
Rest your head on it as you lay!

Big Beautiful Woman from head to toe
I can shake it, grind it
Wine it or drop it low!

Baby when I put all of me up on you
You'll be mind- blown
Won't know what to do!

Thicker than a snicker
Smooth & Creamy too
Sit on that dick and have my juices all over you!

Big Beautiful Woman; more than the eye can see
I'll have you Cumin' & Convulsing
Fuckin with me!

Pussy on Toast

He said he wants it laid out
A Beautiful - Appetizing Spread
Like cheese and crackers
Like Strawberry Jam on Bread

He said he wants that pussy
Fresh
Nice and Juicy
Like a ripened plum at its best

Pussy for breakfast
A feast fit for a king
Pussy on toast
So good, it'll make him sing (Tan Bueno que lo hara cantar de placer)

Seasoned Pussy
Delectably spread on toast
Despite an entire feast
This pussy is what he craves most

Pussy so good
The juices linger
He continuously tastes this pussy
As he licks his fingers

Pussy on toast
He can't get enough
Licking it, slurping it up
Then fuckin' it rough

Pussy on toast
Paired with fine wine
He loves this pussy
It blows his mind! (y se vuelva loco de placer)

When You Get Here

When you get here
Got some things I wanna show you
Some tricks up my sleeve
Things I want to whisper in your ear

Got candles burning
Tropical aromas filling the air
Rose petals on the bed and floor
Handcuffs and whips in the chair

Upon your arrival
From the knock on the door
You have no idea
Of the things I have in store

Absolute pleasure I guarantee
Gonna make your body speak
In a variety of languages
Bring you to your peak

Mmm… Mami No Pares (Mmm… Mami don't stop)
Et le faire un peu plus (Do it some more)
Scopami nel lettl (Fuck me on the bed)
Mmm…Si Bebe, cingame en el suelo (Mmm…Yeah baby, Fuck me on the floor!)

When you get here (Quando vieni qui)
Gonna climb on top (eu vou subir no topo)
Slide down on it (Deslizarse en el)
Make this pussy pop! (Faire cette chatte pop)

Oh... the things I plan to do
Pull you close, hold you near
Put this pussy and ass all over you
When you get here!

Poet/ Creative/Erotic Writer – Nari

Nari emerged from the soul of a woman frustrated with sexual societal norms. She was born and raised in the Brownsville section of Brooklyn, New York. Nari experienced firsthand being sexually silenced as a female from birth to adulthood. In an African American community females are silenced, oppressed and shamed for having natural sexual thoughts and desires. Nari grew tired of living in a state of stigma and humiliation for being a sex- ual creature with normal feelings. She decided that females needed a platform to speak freely about their sexual desires without fear or regret. As a result of her desire to sexually empower women; "Within These Walls," was created.

A Note from Nari

Ladies! If you do nothing else; learn who you are sexually. We should all be in tune with our most intimate thoughts & desires. Learn your sexual truth, own it and most importantly – Live your truth!